CARTOONIA

BOOK 2

Scarlett Harrington Press

***

Published by:

Copyright © 2020 by Scarlett Harrington

ISBN:9780993550997

Table of Contents

PROLOGUE

Rebecca could feel the rays of the sun on her face as the curtain blew from the window. She donned a smile, always a fan of the rays of light on her porcelain skin. Another thing she was a fan of was the touch of men. Strong, male arms wrapping themselves around her as she slept. At the moment, as the sun roused her from sleep, arms were still around her. And each one slowly inched away as she raised herself up on the bed.

"Good—good morning, Rebecca," Ron, one of her lovers, greeted, his blue eyes fixating on her naked breasts.

She didn't bother to look down at her body. She was always naked before going to bed. "Good morning," she greeted back.

He smiled and rolled over, giving her room to step out of bed. As soon as her foot touched the wooden floor of her home, Jer, her other lover, roused away and blinked at her. "You are awake?" he asked.

Rebecca nodded and slowly made her way to the window. She drew the curtains widely open and closed her eyes, feeling the full rays of the sun on her entire body. Her nipples hardened in response to the warmth while her toes curled in ecstasy. When she opened her eyes, her attention drew to the view of the daffodils that surrounded her home. The beautiful plants with trumpet-shaped flowers shone beautifully beneath the sun. Their pleasant smell filled the air, getting her to close her eyes again and imagine how awesome it would be to be sprawled, completely naked, on the field. The plants could caress her tender skin if they wanted, and she would open her thighs and let the rays of light tone her pussy lips and drive her to the edge of climax.

She knew it was all just her imagination, but she couldn't help but smile at the thought of nature, making love to her. For many years now, the two men in her room made love to her in rather unspeakable ways. They fucked her morning, afternoon, and night. But her body seemed to crave more…to long for new pleasure, perhaps from someone else – she might never know. It wasn't as if there were many people in the world that they all lived in now.

As if her lovers could read the thoughts that plagued her mind, both of them stepped out of bed and made their way to the window, too. Ron stood by her left and stood so close, she could feel his cock rubbing against her hips. Jer stood behind her to her right, getting his cock and stomach to rub against her back. Their flawless bodies, rubbing against hers, sent a spasm of pleasure down her spine. Rebecca closed her eyes again and instinctively reached behind her to grip each of their cocks.

"You want us now, Rebecca?" Ron asked.

Rebecca wanted to shake her head. She wanted to tell them how much she desired new men, new cocks, and a new sexual experience. But her body could never deny the unbreakable lust between all three of them. She was bound to them as they were bound to her. And whenever they were willing to satisfy her, she would always give in to them. The same happened to them. She could ask to fuck each man every hour, and they would always become her sex slaves.

With her body giving in to fiery lusts within her, she nodded to Ron's question. And instantly, both men closed in on her as if she was their prey. Jer buried his head into her neck, sniffing her skin and kissing her on her cheek and chin. As for Ron, he plastered his body to her side, reaching for her breasts and squeezing each one to full arousal.

Rebecca reached over her shoulders to hold each man by his neck. Then, she guided them to stand in front of her, slowly bring their head down to her breasts. Instinctively, Ron, and Jer took her nipples into their mouths. They sucked hungrily, getting her body to reel with pleasure.

Eventually, Jer took control of her breasts while Ron knelt down to caress her abdomen and thighs instead. He parted her thighs with his palms, tracing kisses along her groin before focusing on her pussy lips. He used his tongue expertly, diving into her pleasure hole, and waking pent-up desires. Instantly, Rebecca ran her fingers through his hair, holding him in place while ramming her cunt against his lips. He welcomed the move by clutching her butt cheeks and helping her thrust so hard against his face. Then, positioning himself right, he stuck out his tongue, getting it in and out of her squirming cunt with so much joy.

As for Jer, he kept on sucking and nibbling on her breasts. His hand squeezed one breast, and his lips feasted on the other. Rebecca kept his attention on her by holding on tight to his cock. The war meat grew hard and fat in her palm. And as it did, she squeezed and stroked it, earning grunts and moans from Jer.

Eventually, she decided that she had had enough with neither of them already pummelling hard inside her with their cocks. "The bed," she whispered, already feeling a climax rising within her as Ron replaced his lips and tongue with his fingers, shoving them in and out of her. "Take me back to bed now."

Neither man argued with her. Ron rose to his feet, taking her with him. He took her into his arms, snatching her from Jer and returning to the bed. A second later, he dropped her easily as if she weighed nothing. Then, he gripped her thighs, held them apart, and prepared to bury his cock deep within her eager cunt.

Rebecca felt it before either Ron or Jer could – a sudden electrifying jolt within the house like a warning…a warning that something bad had happened. When the full wave of the jolt hit all three of them, pain slid through their bodies. Their vision blurred as their head ringed with pain. Ron scampered back on the bed, letting go of her thighs and then gritting his teeth in pain. As for Jer, he fell to his knees beside the bed, holding his head. Rebecca laid on the bed without moving, trying to fight the sting that shot through her spine.

Eventually, it ended – as abruptly as it had begun. Rebecca slowly sat up, staring at Jer and Ron, who still seemed shaken by the sudden dark force.

"Was that—was that…?" Jer stuttered from the floor.

Rebecca didn't wait for him to finish before she nodded her head. "Someone found Areeyah," she whispered. "They found it, and they are on their way to Cartoonia."

"They are on their way here."

CHAPTER ONE

The letters had floated before her eyes before each of their bodies had been drawn into the book. Lily pondered over the letters and the word they formed, letting her eyes observe the tall trees around them as they walked out of the woods.

Everything around them seemed surreal. There were trees, leaves, and a river that went deeper into the woods, but they weren't exactly the typical nature that she had seen before. The trees looked like they weren't without thick barks and roots that dug deep into the earth. Their surfaces looked like smooth panes of ice while the leaves were like ceramic or porcelain plates without blotches. The water looked clean and perfect. Through it, perfectly shaped and shiny pebbles shone as the light from the sun penetrated into the water.

Lily would have assumed that she was in a dream if she hadn't vividly remembered opening her mother's book and finding herself, alongside Jamie, Peyton, and Kyle, in a different world – an alternate universe, Jamie had called it. And speaking of Jamie, she stole a glance at him as he walked quietly behind her, still holding on tight to Peyton's hand. The two had clutched to each other nearly an hour ago, filled with lust, as Jamie plunged himself inside Peyton, over and over again. At the same time, Lily had gotten overwhelmed by a lust she couldn't explain. She inarguably liked Jamie, but her body had surrendered to Kyle, Jamie's friend. She had let Kyle touch her body like no man had ever done and had eventually cried out his name in ecstasy as he buried his cock inside her.

It wasn't as if all four of them could stop the hold that Cartoonia had over them. Yes, she would call the alternate universe that now. At least, she had held on to the book for weeks and somehow understood what it was, even without flipping through a page. One thing she knew now was – the moment she had opened the book, some of its knowledge had coursed through her. She suddenly knew things that she didn't know before.

Lily finally stopped thinking as soon as they all stepped out of the woods onto a lonely, tarred street. She stared around them, pausing to be sure she knew where they were going.

"Lily?" Jamie whispered, stepping forward. For a second, Lily was glad that he finally let go of the redhead he couldn't seem to detach himself from. Jamie stepped towards her and glanced down the tarred road. "Are you sure you know where next we should go?" he asked.

Lily nodded her head. "Yes, I can't really explain, but something seems to tell me we need to find The Anchor."

"The anchor?" Kyle joined the conversation. "Isn't that like a hook attached to a boat to keep it at the shore or something?"

Lily shook her head. "I am not sure I know what it is yet. I only know finding it would get us closer to our goal."

"And what is that exactly?"

That was from Peyton. The redhead stepped towards them, still with a frown on her face. Ever since the book had brought them to Cartoonia, Peyton had been infuriated and impatient. It was obvious that she didn't like what had happened, and Lily didn't want to blame her. She was responsible for opening the book and stealing them away from the world they all felt safe and happy in.

Holding her breath, Lily calmly explained what their goal was. "To find the book which could take us to the other side – the real world," she explained. "It was Jamie's idea that such a book could exist in this reality."

Mentioning Jamie's name seemed to get Peyton in control of her anger. She bit her lips and nodded. "And you could get us to the book?" she asked.

Lily wasn't sure she had an answer to that question. She clamped her lips shut and stared down the tarred street again. Luckily, before Peyton could insist that she answered her question, Kyle stepped onto the street and glared curiously around them. "The cabin," he mentioned. "It was on the university premises. It doesn't look like we are on university grounds in this, uhm, world."

"It doesn't work that way," Jamie cleared his throat. "In one universe, a region could be Paris with the Eiffel Tower. In another universe, Paris could be New York with the Statue of Liberty. Alternate realities could be the same universe and people with the same names. But the lives that people live differ. Their histories and culture could differ…."

"So, we are not on campus grounds?" Kyle interrupted. "Or even in Lansing in this universe?"

"Apparently, we are not," Jamie heaved a sigh.

"We are in Stone Edge," Lily suddenly whispered. She wasn't sure how she knew the name of the town they were in, but suddenly, she could see a cliff somewhere close to them, with the words, S T O N E E D G E, carved on a piece of rock. She felt a cold breeze on her face as well, indicating they were close to the shores of a large body of water.

"Stone Edge? What is that?" Jamie turned to her.

Lily closed her eyes, trying to visualize the cliff again. She couldn't get hold of it at first, with her mind coming across a blank, but when she tried again, she could hear the sounds of waves, chirping birds, and a boat rocking against a cliff.

"There is a boat," she suddenly whispered, opening her eyes. "And a shore."

"Yes, anchor!" Kyle grinned proudly.

"We need to get to it – the boat?" Jamie frowned.

"Yes," Lily nodded.

"So, where is it – left or right?" Jamie stared at the opposite ends of the tarred road.

Lily followed his eyes, waiting for her instinct to tell her which path they needed to take. "Right," she whispered eventually.

"Good," Jamie responded. "And I hope we could find clean water on the boat or something to eat at the shore you mentioned. I am famished."

"Me, too," Kyle grunted, already walking ahead of everyone else. Jamie trotted after him immediately, happy about the little progress they had made.

Lily made to follow them, but Peyton suddenly placed herself in front of her, her blue eyes staring at her with animosity. "You," she grunted in a low voice. "You made this happen; I don't know how. But Jamie—he is all mine. You let anything happen to him, and you will answer to me."

With that, she was gone, walking behind Kyle and Jamie, as if she hadn't just threatened her.

Lily felt more hatred for the redhead growing inside of her.

CHAPTER TWO

Jamie didn't know how to explain the fear that continued to grip his stomach. He felt stronger and bigger, considering his transformation as soon as he woke up in a world he couldn't even begin to understand, but fear still consumed a part of him. He was afraid that there was a lot they didn't know about the book Lily had opened. More so, they had been walking through the woods for over an hour and hadn't come across a single living thing – either humans like them or even birds and squirrels.

Of course, he didn't want to share this with the rest. He had tried to be optimistic ever since he had realized they were far from home. Asking Lily questions about the book and discussing what they needed to do to get back home seemed like the best option. Talking about the woods, bereft of animals or other humans like them, would only make everyone anxious and mortified than they already were.

With Kyle walking beside him now as they trotted down the tarred road towards the shores Lily had described, Jamie tried to wear a confident smile on his face. Kyle smiled back and stared at his feet, lost in thought. For a second, Jamie tried to guess what could be going on through his mind. A lot had happened in the past twelve hours. First, they had been anxious about attending the born fire. Then they had made plans about drinking and playing games with Peyton in a cabin. The incidents after this weren't something either of them had foreseen. In fact, being transported into the world in a book wasn't something Jamie had ever imagined or thought to be possible.

"Do you think we would ever find our way back home?"

Jamie jolted out of his thought to look at Kyle. "Why did you ask that?"

Kyle heaved a sigh. "Well, we are relying on, uhm, Lily – and trust me, I kinda trust and like her – to navigate through this world. She doesn't strike me as someone who knows here much."

"Yeah, she doesn't," Jamie admitted.

Kyle kept walking but kept his eyes on him as if he was still waiting for a response.

"Yeah, maybe we do not really have a choice than to listen to her," Jamie whispered. "She told us how to get us out of the cabin and also found a way out of the woods. Now, she is leading us…"

"…to the anchor," Kyle finished. "A shore and a boat. Then, what? Will the boat take us to the book, or will it take us home? Do we even know if it is dangerous or safe at the shore?"

Jamie paused to wince at him. "You have a lot of questions, Kyle. I do, too. If we were to wait for Peyton, I am sure she had got questions, too. And no one has the answers, apparently. Lily might look calmer than we all do, but I can bet she doesn't know more than she could tell."

"So…?" Kyle stared over his shoulder at Peyton and Lily, who strolled towards them with a good distance between them.

"So, maybe we should get to the boat first, and then see what happens," Jamie began to walk back. "And I think we are close. I can taste salt in the air."

"Me, too," Kyle frowned, staring frantically around. Jamie noticed him staring at Lily for a second before he made his way down the street back.

"So, you like her, uh?"

Kyle's eyes furrowed. "Like, uhm, what do you mean?"

"You said you trust and like Lily," Jamie expounded with a smile. "And I couldn't help but noticed how passionate you were with her while, uhm…"

"While making love to her, same way you did with Peyton?"

Jamie felt uncomfortable with the topic and cleared his throat. Neither of them was ready to talk about what had happened in the cabin yet.

"Yeah, maybe we should just focus on finding that shore."

"Yeah," Kyle agreed.

Something isn't right.

Peyton could feel anger, spite, and jealousy boiling inside of her. And most of it seemed to be directed at the brunette who couldn't stop stealing glances at Jamie, despite how an hour ago, she had laid naked with another man. It wasn't as if Jamie would ever choose Lily over her; Peyton tried to convince herself over and over again. However, only Lily had all the answers. And often, Jamie had to talk to her than he spoke with her or even Kyle.

She had threatened Lily earlier without thinking twice about it. It was obvious that Lily liked Jamie. She couldn't explain how she knew, but she was a woman, right? Women could sense competition from a mile off, especially if the competition was a beautiful woman who had created a problem only she knew how to solve.

Peyton didn't trust Lily at all. She didn't have any cause to. Everything – getting transported into a surreal world and getting forced to have sex with one another to move out of the cabin – was her fault. Lily probably knew what would happen if she opened the book. And she did anyway. To Peyton, that was not someone to be trusted. Her jealousy and spite apart, she continuously felt a jolt in her guts to be careful around the girl. She wanted to protect Jamie, too, but she didn't know how to.

As they strolled further down the street, she stole a glance over her shoulder at Lily, keeping her close.

Oblivious, Lily continued to stare at the trees around her and then stared down the road as if she was trying to confirm that they were close to the shores.

Keep your eyes on her, Peyton muttered quietly to herself. *She is dangerous, and only you seemed to be able to see through her pretense.*

CHAPTER THREE

"Are you sure anyone found it and are on their way here already?"

Rebecca stood at the shores, staring straight ahead at the distant horizons. The sun had already risen high, and soon, it would be midday. She had expected that their guests would be on the boat, ferrying towards her already, but it seemed that wasn't going to happen anytime soon. She had been standing for nearly an hour, waiting for the sign of the boat but *nothing*. The waters moved restlessly while the breeze blew harshly against her face and dress.

"Yes," she turned to Ron and Jer, who had been staring expectantly at the sea as well. "I felt it. You both felt it, too."

"But we can't be so sure," Ron whispered. "It's been many years since Rachel escaped with Areeyah, swearing to keep us imprisoned here forever. She probably has burnt the book already."

"She couldn't. She wouldn't," Rebecca muttered more to herself than to Ron. She turned back to the sea and stared absentmindedly as the waves picked speed and clashed heavily against the shores.

Although, as Ron had rightly pointed out, it had been many years – more years than she could remember – that Areeyah, the doorway into Cartoonia, had been stolen and carted away, keeping all three of them imprisoned on an island without hopes of seeing their homes ever again. Yet, she didn't want to believe that they were stuck in a surreal world forever. She didn't want to believe that Rachel, the thief, had destroyed their only chance of getting back home.

"No," she grunted, whirling around and facing Ron and Jer again. "Rachel didn't destroy it. The only reason we felt so much pain was because great magic was in place. The magic of the pages of Areeyah being opened again. We felt the same way when we were pulled into this world; you do remember, don't you?"

Ron glanced at Jer and shook his head. "Yes, we do. But a lot of magic happens here as well. It could be that places are shifting again. Various locations are getting turned around to look different. You have seen that happen before. It is only this island and Stone Edge that stays the same, no matter what happens outside their shores."

"Or it could be that Cartoonia is finally destroying itself. We feared this might happen if nothing goes in and out of it for a very long time."

"No," Rebecca spat again, refusing to be pessimistic. "It felt the same. You cannot argue it. You both have just given up that we would ever get back home. You still blame yourself for what happened with Rachel."

Ron and Jer fell quiet immediately. It took a while before Ron stepped forward with his eyes darting emotionally at her. "That isn't fair, Rebecca. We betrayed her first. We all did. Then she—she…"

"She left us here to die," Rebecca heaved a sigh and turned back to the water.

"She left us here to rot while she went back to where it all started as if we never existed."

———

"Hey, here! I think I found the cliff!"

The tarred street eventually came to an end with a very large boulder and bushels, hiding a narrow path to what Jamie could only understand to be the cliff Lily had spoken about.

He stopped in front of the boulder and pointed to the bushels. "There," he directed Kyle, Lily, and Peyton to the path. "Lily, is it the cliff you spoke about?"

Lily walked quietly into the path, fondling with her fingers. At first, Jamie felt that something was wrong with her. She seemed distracted and wouldn't even look into his eyes. At the end of the narrow path, standing at the edge of a cliff overlooking a large shore, Lily finally dropped her hands to her side and turned to look at him and Kyle. "Yes," she whispered. "The shore is the same, too. But I can't find the boat."

"Maybe we need to find our way down to the shore," Jamie suggested, walking down the path towards her.

Lily whirled around, avoiding his gaze again. She searched the cliff and then pointed to some bushels by her right. "There, maybe there could be another path getting us down to the shores over there."

He wanted to hold her and turn her around to face him, so he could figure out what bothered her since the last time they spoke. But looking at the bushels she pointed to, he realized that she was right. Besides, Peyton had appeared beside him to hold his hand. She seemed quite worried as well, and he clutched her hand just to assure her everything was going to be okay.

"Well, we had better head down and find the boat then," Kyle inched forward, making his way through the bushels.

Lily sauntered after him immediately while Jamie paused to speak to Peyton. "You have been awfully quiet," he noted. "I know it is a lot. I mean, I can't even get my head around everything yet. But I am sure we are going to find our way back."

Peyton looked happy that he had thought to comfort her. She placed both her palms on his chest and leaned in to kiss him briefly on the lips. "I am sure we will," she whispered. Then, her eyes furrowed as if she was holding back from telling him something.

"What is it?" he closed the distance between them, holding her hands. "Are you worried that our parents would be searching for us? I haven't even thought about that."

His mother, probably going frantic after losing contact with him for hours, flashed through his mind, and he shook his head to rid himself of the thought. He had refrained from thinking about anyone except himself, Kyle, Peyton, and Lily. They were all that mattered for now until they could find their way home.

"Yeah," Peyton finally responded to his question. She held his hand and made him walk beside her through the bushels to the shore. "Dad and I haven't really been on good terms for a while. I don't want to be stuck here, knowing he would think I disappeared because of him."

He was surprised. Peyton had been so close to her father in junior high school that she had gotten the nickname Daddy's Little Princess. "What happened between you two?" he asked.

"Well, he travels a lot these days," Peyton sighed. "He says it is his job, but I miss the days he was always home. I miss the days it was different with Mum around."

Jamie could feel that they were getting closer to the shore. A fierce breeze blew over his face, and the bushes around them were getting thinner. He nodded at Peyton's statement. "She died years before Junior High, didn't she?"

"Yeah, a long time ago," Peyton smiled sadly. "Before then, Dad was always home. He worked from home and had an office he didn't always want me to interrupt him in. Mum drove twenty miles to her office."

"Hey, Jamie! Come here! We found the boat!"

They had just walked out of the bushes onto the shores of a beautiful, ruffled sea. Across the shores, Kyle was waving his hands in the air at both of them. Behind him and

Lily, there was a boat – no, a sailboat! It was a large sailboat kept at the shore with a rope tied to a tree, which seemed to be out of place on a beach where nothing else grew. The word, ANCHOR, was boldly inscribed on it.

Jamie turned to Peyton with a proud smile. "We found the boat, Peyton. Maybe we are closer to home now. Soon, you wouldn't have to worry about everything back at home. Maybe you could finally get a phone and call your dad."

Peyton didn't seem as elated as he was, but she nodded and hugged him. With her arms letting go of him, Jamie hurried towards Lily, hoping that she knew where next they had to go.

CHAPTER FOUR

Lily saw him heading towards her again. It was stupid to avoid him after Peyton had threatened her, but she couldn't think of any other way. Maybe steering clear of him could rid her of the growing attraction she felt towards him; she also tried to convince herself. But Jamie was really very handsome and friendly. His eyes always bored into hers whenever he spoke, and his smile was the most beautiful sight she had ever seen.

As he walked towards the boat they had found, she noticed how stunning he was, looking buff in tight jeans, a jacket, and boots. It seemed as if the book wasn't satisfied with how handsome he ordinarily was. His beards were blacker and smoother on his cheeks in the alternate world. He also looked taller, and his chest and arms had grown larger and firmer as if he could punch into a rock and not feel a single pain.

An image of her hands running through his jet black hair as he probably gripped her waist and kissed her coursed through her mind. She shook her head to rid herself of the arousing thought. At the same time, Jamie closed the distance between them, wearing a hopeful smile on his face.

Lily instinctively turned around and made her way to the boat. "Hey," Jamie called, trotting after her. "We—we might have to talk about what this boat is and why we had to find it."

She didn't utter a word. She kept walking, using the boat's thick rope and railings to steady herself before climbing aboard its deck. The boat rocked with the ruffled water, and she stood still to keep herself from falling. Surprisingly, the boat was larger than she had seen it in her mind. It had a cockpit for controlling the rudder to sail the boat and stairs that led to a small room beneath the deck. The door into the room was closed, but she knew there were sheets and food beneath it. She had seen them flashing through her mind before she and Kyle had found the boat. There was magic in the world they were in, and it always gave them what they needed.

"Lily," she heard Jamie call before he climbed aboard the boat behind her. "Is everything okay?" he frowned and folded his arms. "I can't, but notice that you are avoiding my gaze."

She turned to look at him, unable to stand how irresistible he was, even when he was confused. The breeze blew against him, ruffling his long hair. "Avoiding your gaze?" she tried to laugh his complaint off, as well as her own endless pinning for him. "I am just worried about everything that has happened."

His eyes furrowed at her, but he nodded slowly and inched towards her. Lily felt her lungs ceasing as he got closer. "You brought us here…I mean, you were made to find this boat for a reason," he said. "It means that we are getting closer to leaving this place," his eyes wandered the sea around them, "whatever it is."

"Cartoonia," she told him.

"What was that?" his eyes returned to her.

"The world we are in," she explained. "It is called Cartoonia."

"Cartoonia," he pondered aloud. "Sounds appropriate."

"Yeah," she smiled. They were all looking like cartoon versions of themselves. Everything around them looked surreal as well. The sea, despite its ruffled waves, looked lightweight and opaque.

"So, Cartoonia," Jamie said, still stepping towards her. "What is it telling you that we have to do next?"

She stared at him for a while, wondering how he could be so calm, unlike Peyton, whom Cartoonia had matched him with obviously. A lot of things could go wrong with her directions, but he had never concerned himself with that. Hope glinted in his eyes as he waited for an answer.

"We sail," she told him. "We are supposed to sail the Anchor to another shore at the end of the sea."

He frowned, obviously at a loss with the possibility of sailing. "Uhm, the sea, it isn't quite still for sailing at the moment. And I don't think anyone of us knows how to sail a boat."

"I can," she replied without thinking.

Her response brought another frown to his face. "You have sailed a boat like this before?"

"No," she said and then shook her head. "I mean, no, I haven't. But yes, I know how to sail this one."

"I don't understand."

She held her breath, trying to find the best way to put it that she suddenly knew how because he had asked. Somehow, Cartoonia gave her the knowledge and the ability that they needed to get from one part of its world to the next.

"I—I," she began, "I just know how to. Since we got here, I know things that I shouldn't know."

He didn't say a word for a while. He only stared at her, lost in thought for a while. Then, he closed the last distance between them. "Maybe that's because you opened the book," he whispered. "And that's good, right? If the book is telling us where to go, and we could abide by these directions, we could be on our way back home."

"Yes, I think so," she whispered in an inaudible tone, already distracted by how close they had gotten on the boat. The breeze struggled through the thin space between them. She could feel her breast tingling beneath her crop top. Her nipples hardened, only a few inches from his broad chest. As the boat rocked with the waves at the shore, she was tempted to sway with it, giving her the opportunity that she needed to smash her body against his.

Unfortunately, Kyle and Peyton climbed onto the boat before she could give in to the temptation. Kyle was still elated about the boat. "It looks big enough for all four of us," he announced. "Has any of you checked the room down the stairs? Maybe we could find something in storage to eat or drink. I don't think there is anything at this shore we could consume."

He scampered to the stairs and shoved the door open. Then, he disappeared into the room. Jamie cleared his throat and stepped aside at the same time that Peyton reached for him. "So, what next?" she asked him.

Jamie's eyes steered back to her, and Lily cleared her throat. "We sail," she repeated. "And we have to do that now before we regret staying here for another minute."

CHAPTER FIVE

Kyle was sure he had seen the desires in Lily's eyes as he climbed onto the boat. Jamie might be oblivious to it, but the brunette had had a thing for him, even before she opened the book and brought them all into an alternate universe. He had seen the way she looked at him in the cabin. Whenever Jamie spoke to her, Lily listened with adoration and respect in her eyes. He had waved these from his thought at first since he had felt unbridled attraction towards Lily the moment he had set his eyes on her.

Of course, they had had sex a few hours after they had met. Lily had clutched on to him with lust as he had buried himself inside her over and over again. But a part of him still suspected that she yearned for Jamie instead. The evidences of her lust for Jamie were always staring at Kyle whenever he saw them together. Often, Lily's cheeks reddened with color, or a smile would dot her face as she looked adoringly at Jamie.

It wasn't as if he was jealous. He couldn't be. Jamie was a good friend; he knew that little about him since they had become roommates. And he was certain that Jamie would never entertain any emotions for Lily since he knew that she was with him.

With him. The thought of that made him roll his eyes and bite his lips as he searched the room in the boat. Because Lily had given in to the lust between them didn't mean that they were *together*. But he wished they were. At least, such a relationship could be the only meaningful thing he could get out of the situation they were in.

Seeing how Lily looked at Jamie had made him sad, but he had quickly hidden his emotions by speaking about the boat. He had hurried down the stairs as soon as Peyton had climbed aboard, too, hoping to get Lily and Jamie to step away from each other before Peyton could see what he had seen. With the conversation above deck now, he was sure everything was fine.

Peyton had asked what next they should do, and Lily had launched into an explanation of sailing the boat before tragedy befell them.

He shook his head in the room. He could feel another tragedy rising between all four of them because of Lily's growing affection for Jamie. He could convince himself all he wanted that it was nothing. If it was *something*, however, it would cause hatred and disunity between them. Peyton obviously liked Jamie and wouldn't let Lily have him. As for him, he liked Lily, too. He would connive with Peyton, if he had to, to make Lily his alone.

He finally found a hole in one of the walls of the room. The sight of bottles of wine and food wrapped in foils made his stomach rumble with hunger. And with his ears picking on Lily's explanation that the sea, despite its stormy waves, would take them where they need to go, he picked up one of the bottles and uncorked it. There were fruits, bread, and meat wrapped in foils – enough to feed all of them the entire week.

He unwrapped a piece of bread and sat against the wall to eat. At the moment, with his body reeling with mixed emotions, he decided that he needed food instead of battling with fear and the disappointment of seeing Lily pinning for Jamie.

He was about to take his first gulp from the bottle of wine when he noticed a small wooden box a few feet from where he sat.

The glistering silver crest on the box drew him in. Moving against his wish, he picked the box, traced the edges of its crest as if it was a prized jewel, and then opened the lid.

The content of the box was something he had never seen before. It was pure, shiny gold and PRECIOUS. With Lily, Peyton, and Jamie's voices suddenly getting louder on deck, he quickly withdrew the box's content and threw it into his pocket.

He returned to his food and kept his lips sealed.

Peyton's eyes went wide in horror. "Hold on," she let go of Jamie and inched towards Lily. "You are saying we need to leave now, in this stormy sea, or risk getting attacked?"

"Not attacked. Forced to leave," Lily corrected. "I don't know how, but I am sure we won't like it."

Jamie shook his head, confused. "I don't know much about sailing, but it is difficult standing still on this boat. And we are supposed to sail?"

"The sea would guide us," Lily argued. "I would like you to trust me."

Peyton began to pace the boat, shaking her head. "Trust? It is suicidal sailing without even knowing where or what we are heading towards. If there is food here…"

"There is food here," Lily interrupted. "Kyle ought to have already found it below deck."

Peyton eyed her and continued. "If there is food here, we can just stay here until the water is calm. We don't have to sail right now."

"You heard me," Lily cleared her throat. "We may be forced to leave."

"Yeah, and everything seems so calm right now, despite how many times you have stated that." Peyton snorted. "You may think you know everything, but you could be out of your mind as well. I---what was that?!"

Jamie heard the loud, shrieking sound as well. He whirled around, staring at the peaceful shore, but there was nothing. The woods, the cliffs – everything was still and quiet. Lily walked to the edge of the boat, frowning. "We— we really need to leave," she whispered.

Peyton still shook her head. She turned to Jamie. "You need to say something."

Jamie shook his head, confused as hell. He wished he could listen to the voice of logic in his head, but his instinct wanted something else. "I think we need to listen to Lily," he whispered, hating the look of disappointment on Peyton's face. "Listen, Peyton," he added. "Lily saw the cliff and the boat, and she brought us here. If she sees something else, maybe we need to listen to her. We can't just wander around, not knowing what to do or where to be."

"But the stormy sea!"

"She says the sea would guide us. And she knows how to sail a boat as well, right, Lily?"

Jamie turned to Lily, but her face had turned into pale white as she continued to stare at the woods. "We need to leave, NOW!" she repeated.

Jamie stopped arguing with Peyton and stared at the woods again. At first, it seemed as if the woods and the cliffs were still motionless and quiet. Then, a wild breeze ruffled the trees and swept through the shores, getting the sea violent within seconds. The boat rocked sideways, getting its rope to tug violently at the tree that kept it at the shore. Another screeching sound echoed around them as if a beast was being roused from within Stone Edge. Jamie and Peyton quickly held on to the railings of the boat.

"Lily?" Jamie gritted his teeth.

"Hey, what was that?!"

Kyle had heard the sound as well. He peeped his head out of the room below deck, looking bewildered. He seemed to have found some food as Lily had said he would. He bit on a loaf of bread in his hand when no one answered his question.

"I should start the boat," Lily grunted above the wind, which was gradually picking speed and was getting loud and fierce. She hopped into the cockpit and threw Jamie a serious face. "We need to leave," she stressed.

"But—but we don't even know what's at the other side of the sea!" Peyton hissed, already getting scared with the sudden violent weather.

"Yes, we don't," Lily roared back, staring intently at her for the first time. "And, I really need you to stop arguing so I can get us back home!"

That shut Peyton up, and Jamie wished there was something he could say or do. He stepped towards Peyton, intending to convince her they didn't have a choice, but another sound echoed from the woods behind them. This time, the ground and the sea shook as if a tornado or a missile was heading for them.

"Into the room, back into the room below deck, Kyle," he yelled. "You, too, Peyton."

He held Peyton by her arm and guided her to the stairs. Kyle had done as he was told without a word. And for a moment, it felt as if Peyton was going to fight him, insisting that she wasn't leaving. When she climbed down the stairs without a word, he heaved a sigh of relief and bent to talk to her above the rising wind. "I am going to help Lily sail the boat," he told her. "Please, don't come up here until everything is safe."

Lily parted her lips to speak, but he bent and smashed his lips against hers briefly. Then, he swept the door close and struggled to get back to Lily. The wind had grown fiercer, and it seemed as if Stone Edge was trying to get them off its shores into the deep sea.

"The rope, Jamie," Lily called from the cockpit. "Cut it loose. I am going to start the boat now."

He stared at the rope, noticing how it still held on to the tree, despite the force of the wind. "How do I cut it loose?" he asked.

"Here," Lily picked up an object from the cockpit and threw it onto the deck beside him. "A knife," she explained. "It looks sharp enough to cut the rope. And be fast. I don't know what would happen if we can't leave here in time."

He nodded, already convinced by their situation. The boat rocked violently at the shore one more time, and he hurriedly picked up the knife and began to make his way off the boat.

"No," Lily yelled behind him. "Just cut the rope halfway. We don't have that much time!"

She was right. A louder shrieking noise took over Stone Edge, getting the earth and water to tumble beneath them. Jamie held on to the railing of the boat to keep himself from falling. And without thinking twice about all the options they had, he staggered to the edge of the ship and began to cut through the rope.

"Faster, Jamie!"

Everything crumbled before him as the knife finally cut through the rope, releasing the boat into the sea. The woods and cliffs at the shores of Stone Edge fell apart, froze, and then imploded, disappearing from his view into a very large hole in the ground.

The boat roared alive just in time, and Lily steered it from the shore onto the ruffled sea towards an unknown destination.

Jamie fell onto his knees on the boat, wondering where the hell Lily's book had brought them.

CHAPTER SIX

Dark clouds had gathered in the sky, and Rebecca was getting impatient. It was going to rain soon, and the sea was getting violent as if something tragic had happened at the other end of it.

Hoping that it wasn't what she thought, she closed her eyes and tried to keep her hopes up by thinking about the first week she had spent in the alternate world of Cartoonia. Then, oblivious to the magic around her, she was happy setting foot into a strange world with Rachel, Jer, and Ron. Ron was everything to her back in their world. They had been dating for a year, and his touch had always left tingling sensations in her sensitive parts.

The weirdest thing had happened when Areeyah had stolen them from their world. It had left unbridled lust in them, and surprisingly, Rebecca had realized that she longed for another man, instead of Ron. It was Jer that her body rippled with ecstasy for. She laid her gaze on him in another world, and she wanted to rid herself of her clothes and beg him to make love to her over and over again.

Cartoonia was a ruthless magical cartoon world that did whatever it wanted. And all four of them had been unable to control themselves against its wishes. The first week was bearable. Rebecca remembered how Ron had resisted the temptation to be with Rachel instead of her. Often time, he took her to a serene part of the woods and kissed her. Promising to fight the magic of the world they had found themselves in, he had tried to make love to her but always stopped midway for fear that the consequence might be catastrophic for both of them.

He was right; it was. Weeks later, after he had given in to his lust and had made love several times with Rachel, he had come to her and had buried himself inside her. Everything had crumbled afterward. Chaos. Betrayal. Hatred. They had all grown apart until Rachel had done the unexpected. She had left them all to perish, stealing their only way back home from them.

Rebecca felt her eyes brimming with tears from the regrets of the past. She opened her eyes at the same time that the sky echoed with the rumbling of thunder. Lightning flashed in the distance, and the waves of the water rustled loudly with the wind.

When there was such fierce weather in Cartoonia, it meant that there was imminent danger. And there was only one way to make it stop – sex.

Rebecca hoped that her guests had it in them to do what was required.

————

"Do you want some food?"

Peyton sat on the floor with her arms around her knees, steadying herself as the boat rocked against the fierce storm of the sea. She was scared and furious. She hadn't signed up to be controlled by a world she barely understood when she had planned to spend bonfire night with Jamie. While she was frantic about everything that had happened, Lily, Jamie and Kyle seemed to be slightly bothered about it all. They were probably used to unexpected or unplanned incidents in their lives, but that was not her. For as far back as she could remember, her life had always played out exactly as her father wanted it to be. He chose where she would school or live, even before he began to move to several towns and took her with him. She had always played by his rules until recently….

"Hey, there is wine, bread, and cheese."

She jolted out of her thought and forced a smile at Kyle, who seemed pretty determined to make her less shaken than she looked. "No, I am fine," she told him.

He bit on the last piece of bread in his hand and nodded. "You know, we are going to find a way out of, uhm, this place," he smiled.

She shook her head at him. "You sound just like Jamie."

"Well, maybe because we both believe there is always an exit out of a tunnel."

"This isn't a tunnel. It looks more like…"

"A maze. A shithole." He finished for her with a tone of sarcasm.

She smiled genuinely at him this time around. "Yeah, I think shithole defines it better."

With a broad smile, Kyle picked up an apple and handed it to her. "You should eat," he said. "Once the boat is sailing peacefully, Jamie and Lily would join us. We could talk about what just happened and why it did."

The possibility of a dialogue between all four of them gave her some relief. She nodded and took the apple from him.

"Go on, take a bite," Kyle urged her with a smile.

She closed her eyes and took a bite, surprised by the rich taste of the apple. When she opened her eyes, Kyle was laughing at her. "Yeah, I imagined the fruits would be as delicious as the wine and bread were. Wherever we are, everything seemed to be perfectly arranged for us. Lily, knowing how we can leave the cabin. Then, the cliff, the boat, and now the delicious fruits, drinks, and food."

"Yeah, and do you have any idea who might be doing all these?"

"It should be what, instead of who?" Kyle shrugged. "There are some powers beyond us here."

"Powers, you mean like magic? A god?"

Kyle shrugged again. "You were out there. I only heard the loud whirring noise. Do you think something could be in Stone Edge that wants us gone because it had had enough of us?"

Peyton wasn't sure she had an answer to that. There was indeed magic or some extra-terrestrial powers in the world they were in. And only Lily seemed to have all the answers. That enraged her.

"Lily," Kyle whispered as if he could read her mind. "She has brought us here, maybe against her own wish, and you don't like that Jamie always turns to her for answers."

"I don't know what you mean."

Kyle blinked at her, obviously convinced that he was right. "You don't have to hate her because of Jamie," he said.

"I don't *hate* her," Peyton tried to argue, but Kyle continued nonetheless. "Jamie wouldn't do anything to hurt you or anyone," he said. "You should know that since you have known him longer than I have."

With that, Kyle pushed a bottle of wine towards her and leaned back against the wall. He closed his eyes with a fulfilled smile on his face, leaving her to munch on the rest of her apple quietly as the boat rocked harder above the sea.

———

Lily tried to steer the boat against the harsh wind. It had suddenly begun to rain, and everywhere looked dark, making it harder for her to navigate towards their destination.

"Jamie!" she called for help, getting Jamie to jolt up from his knees and crawl towards the cockpit. He pocketed the knife she had given to him earlier and hopped in beside her. "What?" he asked. "Are we getting closer?"

"No!" she told him, hating how his presence always made her anxious and out of control. "I can't seem to get the boat on the course that I want. The storm isn't stopping."

Jamie stared around the cockpit, obviously at a loss of how to help. "What do we do?" he asked. "Should we be afraid of tipping over and sinking?"

"No! Oh, no, no," she answered. "There is something we should do. I—I don't know what it is."

Jamie had gotten more confused. He stared above them at the rain and then glanced at her. "Do? You mean to make everything stop?"

She controlled the rudder, getting the boat to avoid a large wave that could have crushed them. "Yes. Yes!" she replied as their bodies rammed into one another with the force of the sea. Jamie quickly scampered back, keeping a little space between them before staring ahead of them at the dark sea. "You said the sea could guide us," he whispered in thought. "Does it feel as if it is doing that now, or doing the opposite?"

"The opposite," she told him. "We are rocking back and forth instead of moving forward."

Slowly, Jamie placed his hands over hers, stopping her from steering the boat. "Then, maybe we really ought to do something," he stated.

She frowned at him at first, compelled by the intent look of lust in his eyes. Then, it dawned on her as his eyes left his face to stare at the door into the room below deck.

"Yes," she whispered. "I think it may be the only way to make it all stop."

41

CHAPTER SEVEN

Jamie made his way down the stairs first and then helped Lily into the room. Peyton and Kyle slowly rose to their feet, trying not to fall as the boat tilted sideways with the wind.

"Uhm, something is wrong, isn't it?" Kyle asked as Lily closed the door behind her. "I don't think we have gotten to the other side of the sea."

Jamie nodded. "No, we haven't. The sea wouldn't let Lily steer the boat across it."

"Then, we go back," Peyton stated.

"We can't," Jamie sighed. "There is nothing left on Stone Edge."

"Nothing left? I don't understand," Kyle stepped forward.

Jamie closed his eyes, trying to get the image of the implosion out of his head. He had never thought something like that was possible. Luckily, Lily closed the distance between her and Kyle to address the question. "Stone Edge wanted us off. When we didn't in time, it destroyed itself."

"Oh, the screeching sound before we left," Kyle muttered.

"So, we are doomed?" Peyton asked, getting their attention back to the current situation. "We can't go back, and we can't head forward either."

"No, we can still get the storm to end and head to shore at the other end of the sea." Jamie inched towards her. "And we know how to do that."

Peyton's eyes furrowed in question and then went wide as she figured it out. "No, no," she whispered. "Not again…" she turned towards Lily, who had already gripped Kyle's hands and had wrapped them around her waist. "We can't stop what Cartoonia wants," she whispered, tipping on her toes to kiss a more bewildered Kyle.

Jamie thought hard about it, hoping there could be another way. He held Peyton's hand and pulled her towards him. "It worked before, Peyton," he whispered, staring at her trembling lips. "Maybe it would work now."

"But—but," Peyton stuttered, already breathless against him. "I don't want it to always be like this."

"Neither do I," he whispered, already feeling his cock rising against her abdomen. "I want to be able to touch you, knowing it is what you and I want."

"And now?" she questioned, her lips already reaching for his. "You don't know if it is what you want?"

He pondered over it, considering how holding and kissing her had been the only thing that had crossed his mind as he thought about a solution to the ceaseless storm. "I don't know if this is me or this—or this world. I just know I want to kiss and touch you again."

Peyton wasn't fully convinced, but she nodded and wrapped her arms around him. Then she hopped onto his arms, wrapped her legs around his waist, and clamped her lips against his.

He kissed her with a grunt, feeling a fiery passion consuming every inch of his body. He was stronger in his cartoon avatar form, so she felt lightweight in his arms as he whirled around and fastened her back to the nearest wall. Peyton's lips tasted of apple and wine. He nibbled on her lower lip gratifyingly and began to search inside of her top and skirt with his hands.

"Oh, Jamie," Peyton gasped as soon as he gripped one of her breasts and butt cheeks. Her body melted against his, waking desires neither of them could stop.

Several feet from them, Lily pulled her crop top over her head and let Kyle's eyes feast on her plump, naked breasts. When he stared lustily at her without a word, she gripped his head and buried his face in between her breasts. Then, she dipped her hand into his pants, stroking his cock, and then gripping it hard.

"Lily," he muffled against her breasts. "I want you. I do."

She paused to bring his head up, so she could look into his eyes. "I want you, too," she whispered, already feeling her clit jolting to the thought of having him deep inside her.

He cleared his throat, shaking his head. "Now the typical want, Lily," he whispered. "I *want* you. I feel the kind of longing that I have never felt before with you. And it isn't just about what this world wants. I feel attracted to you."

His head returned to her breasts, and this time, he picked her up and lowered her onto one of the sheets. Squeezing her left breast in his palm, his lips feasted on her right breast. He nibbled on her nipple button, getting her aroused with his lips, tongue, and teeth. She clutched to his shoulder, stunned by his declaration that he was attracted to her. She had felt connected to him as soon as they had been transported to Cartoonia, but she blamed the magic of the world for that. The only man that she wanted was Jamie, but he wasn't within her reach. He would never be.

As Kyle let out a wild moan and bent to pull up her skirt, so he could feast on her cunt as well, she glanced sideways at Peyton. Jamie effortlessly kept her body against the wall and had ripped off her top and skirt, so he could nibble on her breast and finger her at the same time. Peyton threw back her head and let her body reverberate with pleasure. She let out uncontrollable gasps as Jamie suddenly dropped her to her feet and then whirled her around with her face against the wall.

Lily closed her eyes, trying to focus on her own pleasure. Kyle *wanted* her. And that was all that mattered at the moment. He was the first man who had ever expressed his feelings for her. And she felt some sort of loyalty to him. She returned her palm to his cock as he gripped her jeans and began to pull it down her legs.

Before he could return to her breasts, she flipped him over and climbed atop him. Then, with desires eating into every fiber within her, she slowly inched down and took his rigid cock in her mouth.

Lust. It could be the only way they ever returned home, safe.

www.ingramcontent.com/pod-product-compliance
Lightning Source LLC
Chambersburg PA
CBHW051012050726
47592CB00007B/2811